# ROBERT BURLEIGH

# PANDORA

ILLUSTRATED BY

# RAUL COLÓN

SILVER WHISTLE
HARCOURT, INC.
SAN DIEGO   NEW YORK   LONDON

## AUTHOR'S NOTE

In attempting to reimagine the story of Pandora, I had help from several well-known sources.
The main ones were *The Greek Myths* by Robert Graves, *Bulfinch's Mythology* by Thomas Bulfinch, *Funk & Wagnall's Standard Dictionary of Folklore, Mythology, and Legend* edited by Maria Leach, and *D'Aulaire's Book of Greek Myths* by Ingri and Edgar Parin d'Aulaire.
Although my account follows theirs in its broad outlines, I have naturally added a number of details of my own.

Requests for permission to make copies of any part of the work should be mailed to the following address:
Permissions Department, Harcourt, Inc., 6277 Sea Harbor Drive, Orlando, Florida 32887-6777.

www.harcourt.com

*Silver Whistle* is a trademark of Harcourt, Inc., registered in the United States of America and/or other jurisdictions.

Library of Congress Cataloging-in-Publication Data
Burleigh, Robert.
Pandora/by Robert Burleigh; illustrated by Raul Colón.
p.   cm.
1. Pandora (Greek mythology)—Juvenile literature.   [1. Pandora (Greek mythology).   2. Mythology, Greek.]
I. Colón, Raúl, ill.   II. Title.
BL820.P23B87   2002
398.2'0938'02—dc21   2001001282
ISBN 0-15-202178-7

First edition
A C E G H F D B

PRINTED IN SINGAPORE

The illustrations in this book were done in watercolor and colored pencil on paper.
The display type was set in Sophia.
The text type was set in Meridien.
Color separations by Bright Arts Ltd., Hong Kong
Printed and bound by Tien Wah Press, Singapore
This book was printed on totally chlorine-free Nymolla Matte Art paper.
Production supervision by Sandra Grebenar and Ginger Boyer
Designed by Linda Lockowitz

*For Jenny*
—R. B.

❧

*To Racquel*
—R. C.

# THE STORY OF PANDORA REFERS TO MANY CHARACTERS AND ONE PLACE. THEY INCLUDE:

Aphrodite—the Greek goddess of beauty and love

Apollo—the Greek god of music and poetry

Athena—the Greek goddess of wisdom, war, and handicrafts

Epimetheus—the brother of Prometheus and husband of Pandora

Hestia—the Greek goddess of the hearth

Mount Olympus—the mountain in Greece where the ancient gods were said to live

Pandora—a woman sent by Zeus to punish the human race because Prometheus had stolen fire from heaven

Poseidon—the Greek god of the sea

Prometheus—a Titan who stole fire from heaven and gave it to humans, for which act he was punished by Zeus

Titans—very early Greek gods who were overthrown by Zeus and the other deities who lived on Mount Olympus

Xerxes—a Greek male name, used in this story as the name for Pandora's servant

Zeus—the foremost Greek god and father of all the other gods and mortal heroes

## JAR OR BOX?

Those who study the Greek myths often are undecided about whether Pandora opened a jar or a box. This story follows most of the experts in assuming she opened a clay jar. But either way, the story is the same.

# FOREWORD

It was long, long, long ago. It was a time very different from our time. Before humans arrived, the gods, Titans, and other immortals made Earth their home. Zeus, king of all the gods, charged two Titans, Prometheus and his brother, Epimetheus, with the task of creating animals and the first men. The two brothers went to the riverbank and formed the mortal creatures out of clay. In his excitement, Epimetheus gave the animals many gifts: swiftness, piercing vision, and strength. Too late he realized he had few gifts left for man. Prometheus, feeling sorry for men, stole fire from Mount Olympus and carried it down to them. But Zeus did not want these new, proud creatures to have fire. He punished Prometheus. Then he ordered the gods to create the first woman, the beautiful Pandora, and told Epimetheus that Pandora would be his wife. Epimetheus was pleased. But Zeus was still secretly angry at the mortals who had dared to take what belonged to the gods. He would have his revenge. How? Listen to the story of Pandora and the mysterious jar.

*What was in the jar?*
*The jar that was closed tight*
*And not to be opened!*
*What was in the jar?*
It was all Pandora could think of!

Everywhere else she gazed, Pandora was pleased.
The flowers in the garden,
The porch with its pillars,
The cool smell of marble,
And especially her reflection in the courtyard's still pool.

But one small nagging thought
interfered with her happiness.
What was in the jar?

*Day and night, night and day.*
*The jar!*
*The jar that was not to be opened!*

Pandora.
At the well, bringing the cup to her lips;
Upstairs, closing the wooden shutters
against the bright sunlight.
Again and again it returned:
The thought of the sealed jar!

Pandora.
By the hearth, stirring the coals and
watching the flames rise,
Or under the olive tree,
Poking the thick branches.
But just as the ripe olive tumbled down into her hands—
The thought was back in her mind once more:
What was inside?
What was in the strange, the beautiful jar?

Pandora's husband, Epimetheus,
was firm about this one thing:
*The jar is not to be opened!*
*No.*
*Never. Never. The gods have commanded it.*
*The gods have commanded it!*

See—there it is!
In its own small room just off the courtyard,
There was the jar—high on a pedestal.
It seemed to call out:
*Open me, open me, open me!*

One day, when Epimetheus was off in the fields,
And the house was very quiet,
Pandora did more than peek.

She tiptoed into the room!

Even from far away,
The jar seemed to give off an odd glow.
Its black band shimmered.
Its gold gleamed.
Inching closer, Pandora could see
The two curved handles, like strange staring eyes.
She stopped and stared.

A story was painted on the sides of the jar:
It showed brave Prometheus
Stealing fire from the heavens
And carrying it down to the people.
And there, too, was pitiful Prometheus,

Being punished by Zeus for this very theft.
He was held captive
Until the end of time,
His liver pierced and pecked by a monstrous bird!
Was this a warning to Pandora, too?

Afraid to move in the dimly lit room,
Pandora shivered.
*The gods have commanded it!*
*The jar must never be opened!*
She edged back, step by step.
She turned and, trembling,
Raced from the house.

"Child?"
It was her servant, Xerxes.

"Xerxes," Pandora asked, feeling her calm return,
"Tell me again how I came to be here."
And while Pandora listened,
The kindly old man retold what he could of a strange tale.
He told how the gods had made a perfect creature
of pure clay,
A woman with red ruby lips and shining sapphire eyes;
How the four Winds blew breath into the lifeless figure;
How each goddess and god in turn gave a wonderful gift:
From Aphrodite, beauty;
From Apollo, music;
From Hestia, a gentle soul;
From Poseidon, a love of the deep sea;
And lastly, from Athena, a wish to know all things.

"And they named this first of all women,"
Xerxes continued, "Pandora, the all-gifted.
And so you arrived, my dear, on a bright morning to—"

"But the jar, Xerxes, the jar?"

The old man's gaze darkened.
"The jar?"
Xerxes paused before continuing:
"It was here when you came,
And no one quite knows who brought it.
That is all I am sure of."
He paused again, then whispered,
"Beware the jar, young mistress. Please. Beware."
He shook his head and said no more. . . .

Days passed. Weeks passed.
But Pandora's curiosity about the jar did not lessen.
Oh no, not at all!

Instead, it grew, like a clinging vine,
Tighter and tighter around her waking thoughts.

She tried to forget.
She tried to think of other, simpler things.
She tried to occupy her time.
She stood by the stone wall and sang ancient songs.

She knelt in the courtyard
And with a small brush painted old stories on the white tiles.
But like a map where all the roads lead to one city,
In Pandora's mind,
All the songs and old stories seemed somehow to lead back . . .
To the mysterious, sealed jar.

One day, while strolling in the nearby high hills,
Pandora was troubled by a new thought.
Would the goddess Athena give *her,* Pandora,
The power to think and wonder—
And order her not to use it?
No, it was not possible!

Just at that moment, Pandora glanced up.
Crouched on the rock ledge above her,
A beautiful mountain lioness stared down.
The woman and the animal gazed at each other in silence.
Then the lioness slowly turned
And, with a long, graceful leap, disappeared!

What did it mean?
Pandora could not say.
But on the way home
She suddenly felt more courageous than ever before.

The next morning, all alone in the house,
Pandora paced nervously back and forth.
Each time she passed the jar room, she stopped.
Once. Twice. Three times and—

Quickly, she stepped inside and shut the door.
Couldn't she open the seal just a little—to look?
Pandora crept forward.
Her breath came in short bursts. Her heart quivered.
Yes, no, yes, no—
Yes!

Her fingers trembled as she fumbled with the lid.
She lifted the jar's leather cap and peered in.
The room was filled with a sudden stillness.

Then—*whoosh!*—
she was heaved back as if by a wave.
Dazed, flung against a wall,
She saw dreadful winged creatures flap from the jar.
Twisted-faced things announced themselves.

Pandora heard screaming voices surround her—

"I am War and Anger.
I am death and blood.
I am faces downward
In the thickening mud!"

"I am Falsehoods,
I am Lies:
Wherever I come, you walk
With shrouded eyes!"

Screeches, growls, whistles, hoots.
A gnashing of teeth. Laughter that seemed
To rise from a well of diseased water.
With all her strength, Pandora crawled toward the jar.
A flurry of claws and feathers beat against her face
As the evil ones fled the room.

Pandora reached up with one arm
And snapped the lid back in place.
From deep in the jar, one small distant voice sounded.

"Hope. I am Hope
And I remain,
After the suffering,
After the pain!"

Oh, there was something *good*—and it had not escaped!
All was not lost!
Dizzy and frightened, she staggered outside.
Xerxes came running up to the porch.
"Xerxes, Xerxes," Pandora called out. "The jar—
There were bad things—and they have escaped!"

Dust was swirling. Small birds were fluttering
In confused circles about the trees.
Far off, above the distant peaks,
A black cloud rose and spread its shadowy wings.
A storm was coming. Trouble.

"I know, child. I know, I know!" Xerxes answered.
He grasped Pandora's hand tightly.
"Xerxes," Pandora cried out again,
"It was my fault. What can we do?"

The old servant looked up at the darkening sky.
"Harm and evil are in the world now," he said softly.
"We must be brave, very brave."

Pandora's eyes flashed.
Yes, she *would* be brave!
She would use the gifts and powers that the gods had given her.
She and her people would find a way.
Suddenly Pandora felt her fear lessen.
She felt a lightness lift her spirit like a glistening bubble.
*What is it?* she wondered.
Then she understood.

Hope remained in the jar.
Hope was hers.
And what was more,
She would hold on to it tightly—
As long as she lived.